D0469387

THREE SISTERS

THREE SISTERS

An Emily Castles Mystery

HELEN SMITH

*Sign up for Helen Smith's Book News and get a FREE
Kindle copy of one of Helen Smith's books.
Go here to learn more: http://eepurl.com/ssbf5*

TYGER BOOKS

ISBN: 978-0956517074

For Brenda, Hans and Emily

IN MEMORY OF JESSIE
14th February 1993 ~ 13th October 2010

THREE SISTERS

The south London sky exploded with a thousand deaths that night. Emily looked up. Tiny coloured lights hung in the blackness, like Midget Gems suspended mid-rinse in a toddler's open mouth. She was on her way to the bonfire party at the big house at the end of the street in Brixton, where she lived, at the invitation of the new owner, whom she had never met. Emily should have been used to the fireworks at her age because there had always been fireworks on bonfire night, for as long as she could remember – the fireworks now as much a celebration of Diwali, the Hindu festival of light; and Halloween, the American festival of gore and dressing up; as Guy Fawkes Night, when people in England remembered the day back in 1605 when a plot had been foiled that, had it been successful, would have blown up the Houses of Parliament, with King James I inside it.

But tonight each explosion startled Emily slightly, as if it was the sound of a gunshot, danger. And the sizzling sausage smell of blackening flesh that hung in the autumn air made her think of her dog, Jessie, who had died the week before. The dog had not been barbecued: she died peacefully, after a long and happy life. But she had very much enjoyed eating sausages.

Emily was carrying a tray of homemade cheesy potato bake – a wholesome, portable dish that usually went down well at parties – and a bottle of rosé wine. Ordinarily she wouldn't have gone. Ordinarily, she would have been at home with Jessie, just in case the dog was disturbed by the noise of the fireworks. But those days were gone. And when the handwritten invitation had been slipped through her letterbox, well, she had interpreted it as a sign that she should start a new life and find some new friends. How was she to know she was making an appointment, not just with a new life, but with death?

Halloween had fallen this year on the weekend before bonfire night, and as usual, many people were out celebrating both events. Local children wandered the streets in ugly masks. At least, she hoped they were masks. For a moment or two Emily felt uneasy – what if this invitation was some sort of trick? What if she got to the big house at the end of the street and the place was dark and deserted? But then she seemed to feel the presence of her dog, Jessie, walking beside her for a few paces, and she felt reassured.

As she got closer to the house, she saw it was not deserted. First she heard music, and then she saw the coloured lights strung up in the trees, and finally she heard the happy buzz of conversation from people gathered in the garden. The guests were easily distinguishable from their hosts because they wore anoraks, scarves and gloves. The hosts were walking on stilts or juggling fire – the first sight Emily had was of a giant, glowing, pink papier-mâché or fibreglass painted head floating about five feet above the top of the privet hedge that surrounded the property.

Like most people who live in London, Emily didn't know her neighbours very well, though she knew most by sight and some by name – usually because she'd had to take in parcels or bouquets of flowers when they were out. She recognised Dr. Muriel walking through the gates just ahead of her, pulling a small two-wheeled shopping trolley with one hand and tapping at the pavement for support every three or four paces or so with an elegant silver-topped cane in the other. Dr. Muriel was a hearty, squarish woman the colour of concrete. She lived in one of the red brick Edwardian houses opposite Emily's flat. Emily had taken in mail order deliveries of large parcels of nutritious bird seed from the RSPB for Dr. Muriel. Now, as she followed her, she imagined Dr. Muriel standing very still in her garden with her cupped hands outstretched, wild birds perched along her sleeves as if she were a washing line, waiting their turn to peck at the sunflower seeds and other delicious avian titbits while their benefactor cheeped and chirruped to them in a language they seemed to understand. Though it would have been a sight to behold, Emily had never seen anything like this happen, she only imagined it.

To her left, as Emily walked into the garden where the bonfire party was being held, she saw a monkey puzzle tree strung with coloured light bulbs, as dangerous – with its sharp prickles and damp electric wires – as a cheaply-made, faulty, imported, artificial Christmas tree. Next to the tree stood a tall, thin woman with curly hair, who was another neighbour of Emily. Emily knew her name was Victoria and she had three male children who were fond of skateboarding. Victoria was preoccupied with chasing a cube of potato salad across a cream-coloured cardboard plate with a fragile-looking white plastic fork. She didn't look up when Emily passed. One of her duffle-coated children stared out at Emily through a wolf mask while bending his knees and sliding his back up and down against his mother's trouser leg, like a donkey relieving an itch on a fence post. Without taking her eye off her meal, his mother bent and murmured something to him, and he stood still and looked up at her and away from Emily.

It was a very cold, dark night, and the air was damp, but there was no rain. The conditions were perfect for the party, and the garden was filled with people determined to enjoy themselves, clumped near the fire bowls and coloured lanterns for warmth and light, and ooh-ing and aah-ing at the stilt-walkers and jugglers. They swapped spurious, conflicting pieces of information: the stilt-walkers were Polish, the jugglers were Scottish, the artist who had made the giant head was Spanish, it was a squat party, it was illegal, it was sanctioned by the local council, it was bankrolled by Sir Paul McCartney. Most of it was nonsense, but some of it was true.

A man and a woman Emily didn't know stood at the bottom of the three or four stone steps that led up to the door to the house, sipping at cinnamon-scented mulled wine from white plastic cups and smoking cigarettes. They smiled at Emily as she passed, and she saw that the woman's lips were painted red, and her teeth had been stained the colour of blackberries by the wine. Her brown fuzzy hair had been teased into an unflattering triangular shape, and she seemed to have pencilled her eyebrows in without looking in a mirror.

'If you want the baby,' said the man to the woman, 'have the baby. Or sell it. I don't care.'

The woman shrieked. She seemed deranged. The man dropped his cigarette and grabbed at her. Emily stopped on the top step and turned, ready to intervene. But the woman let him put his arms around her. She smooched with him, rubbing the fox fur collar of her long black coat against his shoulder, and the two of them turned slowly in each other's arms, like lovers dancing on a music box, as she began to sing the chorus of 'La Vie en Rose'. People standing nearby recognised the tune and came a little closer to listen. Some of them clapped. Emily moved on.

Inside the house was a grand hall so large that it was served by two staircases. The plaster on the walls was cracked, and there was a slight smell of mildew, but the flagstones on the floor had been scrubbed, and the place had been fixed up with chandeliers hanging from the ceiling and original artwork on the walls. A man in a cape and a top hat swooshed past – he was young, no more than twenty-one or twenty-two, and he was wearing a false moustache, and he had rouged his cheeks. He tipped his hat at Emily. 'Madame,' he said. Emily smiled weakly. A heavy wooden door opened on the opposite side of the hall, and as two laughing teenage girls emerged, Emily saw that they had come from the kitchen, and she headed there to leave her offerings.

The kitchen was bare, pretty much, except for a large porcelain sink and a cream-coloured fridge that was taller than Emily and twice as wide. And there were two trestle tables, one stacked with bottles of booze, a large pot of mulled wine that was being heated over a small portable gas burner, and a bowl of punch. The other was laden with dishes prepared by the hosts or brought by the guests: macaroni cheese, mince pies, quiches, pasta salads, rice salads, tuna salads, potato salads, baked potatoes, garlic bread – and an assortment of minced pork, beef and lamb products in the form of sausages, scotch eggs, a cottage pie, and chilli con carne. Everything was on the spectrum from brown to cream, and the overall effect was of a sepia-toned display that had been put together by someone nostalgic for a time before Britons had learned to cook, but after they had learned to shop at supermarkets.

'What a spread!' said Dr. Muriel, with the jovial sincerity of a popular visitor to an old people's home or a primary school. 'Wouldn't it be fun to try and guess who has brought what?'

Emily edged her cheesy potato bake onto the table next to the scotch eggs, thinking it wouldn't be fun at all; her dish had already congealed slightly, and the top was glazing over, as if she had persisted in telling it a very dull story on the way here. From her trolley, Dr. Muriel brought a bottle of port, two dozen homemade mince pies and a large round Stilton cheese. 'Low self-esteem is often caused by low blood sugar,' she said, filling a plate with a selection from the buffet. 'It's a good idea to eat well at parties.'

A young woman in a belted mac approached Emily. She was very, very thin with dark, short hair held back with a clip with tiny glass beads on it that nobody could possibly have mistaken for real jewels, and she came so close that Emily could smell the wardrobe smell on her coat. The flesh under her cheekbones was scooped out, like a jack-o'-lantern, but prettier.

'My name is Elise. Can you help me? I need to get a message to our friend, but I'm being watched. I have information that is vital, *vital*, to the success of our joint endeavour.'

Emily looked around uncertainly, and then she looked back at Elise, who was staring at her intently.

'What's the message, m'dear?' asked Dr. Muriel.

'The message is in the suitcase.'

'And who's it for? Who's our friend?'

Elise looked surprised at the question. 'Why, the gentleman who is waiting for the suitcase, of course.' She turned to leave. Then she stopped and held up one finger. She looked at Emily. 'Could you help me get the suitcase to the gentleman?' she asked.

Emily said, 'Well, I...' She shrugged. Then Elise shrugged – she might have been mimicking or mocking Emily. 'Maybe later,' Emily said.

Elise gave her a look of such desperate longing that Emily felt embarrassed. Elise turned and walked away, moving slowly, with dignity, like someone who is used to being watched.

Dr. Muriel looked for somewhere to put her plate down so that she could applaud as Elise walked away. There was no space on the trestle table so she held on to the plate and thumped the top of her left hand with her right, as if she were trying to knock clods of mud from her wellington boots. Marvellous!' she said. 'Marvellous!'

At the door that led to the grand hall, Elise turned and inclined her head. Then she was gone. Even though it had only been make-believe, Emily still felt involved, guilty.

More guests came into the kitchen. Some were wearing fancy dress – but even when their costumes were hired, the guests were easily distinguishable from their hosts. Their hosts moved purposefully through the rooms like characters pouring into the party from an alternate world, obeying rules and impulses and reacting to events and objects that only they could interpret, whereas their guests were just ordinary people who were standing about, enjoying the various 'entertainments', but contributing nothing.

It was somehow a metaphor for life, but Emily couldn't see what she was supposed to learn from it. She was too old to run away and join a theatre troupe. Anyway, for now, something else was bothering her. 'I never know what to say or even if we're supposed to join in.'

'Nerve-wracking, isn't it!' said Dr. Muriel. She didn't look nervous at all; she looked as if she could stand and face a charging rhino.

Emily left her and went to explore.

The dilapidated house had been done up quickly and efficiently at very low cost, furnished with furniture from skips and material salvaged from jumble sales, and decorated with original artworks created by members of the collective who had occupied the place. Emily's favourite so far was an oxidised metal sculpture of the skeleton of a horse. It seemed to be galloping along one of the balconies, where Emily had looked up and seen it from the ground floor.

Nails and staples were visible in the furnishings if you looked close up, but from a distance the effects were grand, theatrical, striking. Emily was impressed with the transformation – she had often walked past on her way to work, head down, not looking forward to her day, or head down, hurrying to get home again to Jessie. If she had thought about the house at all, she had only thought that it was a shame that the place was slowly rotting away. Now she could see that something wonderful had been achieved with determination and an entrepreneurial spirit. Was it because they were risk-takers? Was it because they had gathered here from all over the world, a group of culturally diverse people pooling their resources harmoniously to achieve success? Emily climbed the stairs to have a look around on the first floor. From what she had observed at the party so far, most of her hosts were engaged in dangerous activities – walking on stilts, juggling with fire – of the kind that she had been warned against as a child. Had they never been warned? Was she seeing the product of neglectful childhoods? Or was she witnessing a collective rebellion? Whichever it was, she was astounded by the results.

Even as Emily was pondering this, a young woman came running up behind her in a corridor with *not just one* but a dozen knives in her hand. Emily stood very still, a deer in a forest. But the woman ran past. She was a slim woman – young enough to be called a girl, still – with dyed blonde hair. She was wearing a blue-grey spangled circus-style costume that was rather tatty close up – stained under the armpits, slightly frayed at the groin, and with loose threads where sequins were missing.

The knives she was carrying had short, stubby blades and ornate handles – probably they'd be better described as daggers, rather than knives. The girl ran full-tilt into one of the rooms further along the corridor. Emily followed, curious. Perhaps there was to be another entertainment. Emily opened the door and peeped in. The room had been done out like a frou-frou boudoir, with swathes of pink velvet draped above a very large bed, gilt mirrors on the walls, and a fancy white and gilt dressing table with a very large hole smashed in the side, as if someone had kicked it. That was the only clue that it might have been rescued from a skip (though, of course, it could have been damaged recently in an argument). The gilt mirrors were spotted and cloudy, and their frames were chipped. But at a glance, the decorative effect was decadent and appealing. The girl with the knives lay on the bed – the knives were in a box next to her. She looked thunderously angry, registering emotions of the sort of intensity that might easily have resulted in a piece of furniture being kicked. Another blonde girl in a slightly less tatty blue-grey costume sat on a pink velvet-upholstered chair in front of the dressing table. She touched up her make-up, leaning in toward the gilt mirror propped above it, flicking at her lashes with mascara, her lipsticked mouth a pornographic O. Emily noticed that there were surprisingly few things on the dressing table – just a hairbrush, a jar of foundation, a big pink pot of blusher with a long-handled brush to apply it, and an uncapped red lipstick in a gorgeously old-fashioned gold casing.

At first sight, because of their matching costumes, hair colour and make-up, the two girls looked almost identical, but as Emily looked from one to the other, she began to see differences – this one had higher cheekbones, that one had fuller lips, and so on. It was disconcerting because the dressing room mirror was angled so that Emily could see into it from the doorway. The result was that Emily could see three near-identical faces, though there were only two sisters in the room.

As Emily was gawping at the sisters, the door to the en suite bathroom opened to the boastful sound of the toilet flushing, and Emily's Japanese neighbour Midori stepped into the bedroom. The flushing continued loudly. It sounded like applause. Midori certainly deserved it: She was wearing white

PVC hotpants, long white clumpy boots, white eyeshadow, pale pink lipstick. She came towards Emily with a smile, shaking her still-damp hands as if she hadn't been able to find the guest towel. Even if she'd improvised by wiping her hands on her clothes, as Emily might have done, there would have been no point: she was wearing nothing absorbent.

The sisters looked up at Midori, apparently unaware that she'd been using the facilities, and then they looked at Emily. They didn't seem pleased to see either of them.

'Zizi!' said the girl with the knives to her sister.

Zizi got up from the dressing table. As Midori stepped out of the bedroom past where Emily stood gawking in the doorway, Zizi shut the door in Emily's face. It seemed unnecessarily rude – but then again, it could have been part of a performance.

'Heh!' Emily said to Midori, by way of acknowledging that this place was exciting, but also really rather unsettling.

Midori said, 'Emily, right?'

'Yeah. We live on the same street.'

'I seen you with your dog. Very old.'

'She died.'

'Oh. I'm sorry, Emily.'

'That's OK. You look nice, Midori. I wish I'd dressed up a bit.'

'I'm DJ. I'm playing tonight – only neighbour involved in the party. Very exciting.' She twisted her hands and linked her fingers together, and then she moved her hands up and down a few times, as if attempting a handshake of self-congratulation.

'Hey,' said Emily. 'That's great, Midori!'

'I got a DJ stage name: "Hana-bi" – Japanese name. You know what it means?' Emily obviously didn't look like much of a linguist because Midori didn't wait for her to reply before supplying the answer. '"Fireworks". The words say "fire flowers."'

'That's lovely.'

'I'm on in a half hour – going to the kitchen to have a bite to eat. You wanna come?'

'Yeah, why not? Food's always comforting at a party.'

'Those sisters upset you, Emily? Very rude.'

'No. It's fine.'

So Emily went down to the kitchen with Midori to have a bit of food. The kitchen was crowded this time, with people lining up to put food on their plates. Emily cheered up a bit, and then she saw that her cheesy potato bake hadn't gone down well. It was rather grey and congealed, and she overheard one of the other revellers being rather rude about it. She recognised him as one of the Australian lads who lived on her street.

'What do you make of that, Jake?' he said to his friend.

'It's proof of life on the moon,' said Jake. 'It *is* made of cheese – and grey rocks. And some scientist is gonna be sorry his wife has raided his lab and brought a sample of his work to the party instead of the shepherd's pie she was supposed to bring.'

'Oh, hey, shepherd's pie? I wouldn't mind some of that. Can you see any? Wahey, Chris! Great party.'

This last remark was addressed to a fair-haired English man who was eating a green apple. He nodded.

'Midori,' said Chris. 'You're all set up outside, whenever you're ready. You OK for food?' The pyramid of food teetering on Midori's plate suggested that this was so. 'You want a drink? You want a glass of punch?' He ladled some punch into a paper cup and handed it over. 'How about your friend?'

'Emily,' said Emily. 'No, I don't think so. Thank you.'

'Chris is in charge,' said Midori. 'Party's his idea.'

'So you sent the invitation?' said Emily.

Chris said, 'Not personally.'

'I didn't expect you to be English. I thought everyone in this... collective... was Spanish or Polish or...'

'Yeah. All except me.'

'So you all chipped in to buy this place?'

'We don't go in for ownership. We've got a network around the world to help us identify abandoned spaces. We identify, occupy, beautify – we fix it up and make one little corner of the world a prettier place. And then we move on. We've been on the road for a long time.'

'And now you've come home,' said Emily.

'Home?' said Chris. 'Home is where the art is, Emily.'

He had an intense way of looking at her, as though he was assessing her worth – and had found her wanting. She didn't like his slightly sardonic way of talking. She found she disliked him. But what was it she objected to? His intensity or his flippancy? Or just the way he looked at her. She hated to admit that there was nothing intellectual about her reaction – she was probably just out of sorts after overhearing Jake's comments about the food she had made.

Emily wanted to get away from the kitchen, but Chris was still here, hemming her in by the buffet. 'Are you enjoying the party?' he asked.

'I am. I never know what's going to happen next.'

'It's all great. Just don't miss the knife throwing.'

'Is that the sisters? Zizi and...?'

'Zizi and Zsa-Zsa. They're awesome.'

'Yeah. They didn't think much of Midori using their bathroom while they were trying to get ready.'

'Did she? Where was that? Upstairs?'

'I tried to get a look in case it was a performance, like Elise–'

'Ah, poor Elise. I wonder if she's got anyone to take her suitcase to that man yet.'

'She asked me. Was I supposed to say yes?'

'Yes.'

'So which one is it who throws the knives? Is it Zizi or Zsa-Zsa?'

'You'll have to see it to find out,' Chris said. He looked amused.

'There's no audience participation, is there? They both looked in such a mardy mood just now, I don't think I'd want to take my chances.'

Chris smirked. The expression made his nose look very long and straight, and his mouth looked strangely sexy. Emily thought she had detected in Chris's accent and demeanour a sense of entitlement that only comes from rich, well-educated people – the sort who can afford to go swanning off around the world with a troupe of performers in the name of art. *If you were really so well brought-up,* Emily thought, *you might ask 'do you mind if I smirk?' before puffing your condescension all over me.* But then she remembered her dog had just died, and probably that was making her thin-skinned and emotional, and she was at a party, and she seemed to have forgotten how to enjoy herself, and she had better start.

And then a tall, dark-haired man edged in next to her at the buffet table and took charge of things, as though he had heard her silent command to get the party started. 'Joe,' said Chris, nodding in acknowledgement. Was there a hint of antagonism in the way he said Joe's name?

'OK, man,' Joe said. He was strong-looking, as though he worked outdoors, and he spoke with a slight accent. He turned away from Chris, and as he turned away – he was half a head taller than Emily, so she had to tilt up to get a good look at his handsome face – she saw something she hadn't been expecting to see in response to Chris's antagonism. Not bitterness or aggression or anger or indifference. No, for a moment she thought Joe looked sad.

'You got to eat something,' Joe said, noticing Emily's empty plate. He put a huge spoonful of her cheesy potato bake on her plate, and then he put an equally good portion of it on his. 'It's good,' he said, as if she needed persuading. 'We make it like this at home in Hungary. You have the meat, and you have the potatoes. I don't understand this *layers* of things,' he indicated the dish of lasagne and the dish of cottage pie, 'like they want to hide the meat in there because it's shy.'

He looked towards Midori, but her plate was full. She stood and scoffed her food right there in the kitchen in a ladylike but extremely efficient manner, plate to her chin, fork to mouth, fork to mouth, fork to mouth. With her crazy white gear and her repetitive movements, she could have been a next-generation robot demonstrating hoovering techniques.

'Ah. Better,' she said when she was almost done. She put her plate down and used both hands to snap the heads off two prawns that remained on it, then sucked the meat out of the prehistoric little bodies like a very genteel predator.

'You want some punch?' Joe said to Midori. He put a paper cup down on the table next to her.

'Got some.' She took an individually-wrapped, alcohol-soaked hand wipe from the pink plastic bag that was slung over her shoulder, the cartoon cats depicted on it bouncing at her hip, and she ripped open the packaging and carefully wiped all eight fingers and two thumbs on her hands like a proud mama. She swigged the cup of punch down in two draughts, and then she went out into the garden where her DJ booth had been set up.

Joe loaded up his plate with meatballs and salad, and every time he took something for himself, he first offered a serving of it to Emily. He took two paper napkins and two plastic forks from the table. He said, 'You want to go outside and eat?'

Emily did. She had formed rather a good first impression of Joe, with his strong, muscular arms and his air of slight sadness. Added to that, he had been nice about the food she had brought.

Emily and Joe went and sat together on two plastic chairs in the enormous garden. It was much bigger than any of the other gardens Emily had glimpsed from her street. It was much bigger than her garden, which she tended lovingly in spite of the difficulties of maintaining a lush green lawn that arose from allowing an elderly Golden Retriever to piddle on the grass a couple of times a day.

The party house had once been a very grand house, and the size of the garden where Emily and Joe were now sitting was testament to that. There was a small orchard off to the west of the garden, with apple, cherry and pear trees in it. Nearer the house were neglected flower beds with overgrown shrubs and bushes, and midway between house and orchard, on what had once probably been a very fine lawn, there was a towering bonfire that had not yet been lit. It was stacked with sawn-up pieces of wood, branches and kindling. Emily surmised that it had been built by a man because in her experience men were good at making fires (goodness knows, she was self-sufficient, but building a decent fire in the grate in the decorative but functional tiled fireplace in her flat was the one thing she never quite managed to do to her own satisfaction).

Close to the house was Midori in her DJ booth, a temporary structure decorated with fairy lights and bearing a hand-painted sign with 'DJ Hana-bi' on it. Closer still was a barbecue with a man in a chef's hat, an apron and checked trousers. He was carving roast pork from a pig on a spit and serving it to a very long line of hungry customers. Emily wondered if there was any difference, ethically, between eating a dog and eating a pig. If so, then whether or not it was acceptable to eat a two-year-old child was another question that ought to be considered as part of the mix: Emily had read that dogs were supposed to be just as intelligent as toddlers, and she had read that pigs were cleverer still.

Emily didn't think she ought to share with Joe her thoughts about pigs, dogs and toddlers. She didn't want to allude to her assumption that he must be good at lighting fires as he was a man. She didn't want to sit there and imagine him chopping up pieces of wood with an axe in his hands. She didn't want to sound as though she was being suggestive or simpering at him.

'Did you build that bonfire?' she asked Joe.

'I helped,' he said.

She pressed on, trying to find a bonfire-related question that didn't involve a mention of chopping, smoking, lighting fires... she came up with, 'I hope you checked for hedgehogs this morning, if it's been there overnight. You know, they crawl in there and sleep if it looks cosy?'

'Hedgehogs, horses, people. We checked it, don't worry. When they light it, there's gonna be a big parade. They're gonna put an effigy on the fire and burn it. You're gonna stay and see it?'

'Oh, yes. And the knife throwing. I want to see that, too.'

'Yeah? Why?'

'I heard it was good. Zizi and...'

'Zizi and Zsa-Zsa. Crazy girls. Yeah, it's one hell of an act.'

'What do you do here... Joe?'

'Joszef. You can call me Joe.'

'Do you have an act, Joe?'

'No, Emily. It's Emily, right?'

She was eating a meatball, but she bobbed her chin up and down, acknowledging that he was right.

He said, 'I don't put on a mask. I make some of the props. The art works – did you see the metal horse upstairs? I made that. I used to be a blacksmith in my hometown. So now I do this.'

'Where's home?'

'Hungary. What about you, Emily? You from here?'

'Yeah, I'm... I'm one of the neighbours. One of the guests. I live on this street. I'm not from London, though. But this is a city of immigrants, isn't it? Nearly everyone's moved here from somewhere, including me. Though I only moved from the countryside – no need for a passport.'

'You OK, Emily?'

'Do I look miserable? My dog just died.'

'Oh, that's a shame.'

'Well, everyone who has a dog; it dies eventually. I just need to get over it.'

'That's OK – it just happened... didn't it?'

'Yes. And I've been moping about the house the last few days, and I realised I'd been operating for years as one half of a human/dog duo. I need to get used to life without the furrier half. The separation is so real, I can feel it. If you had a diagram of the human body here now, I could point to the place where the wound would run from just beneath my armpit to just above my thigh – as if there was some kind of physical manifestation of the separation from Jessie.'

'I don't have a diagram of the human body, Emily.'

'I don't have any outward scar.'

'Oh, OK. I wondered if you were going to ask me whether I wanted to see it.'

Emily thought, *Are you flirting with me, Joe?* She blushed. She looked at his neck where his shirt was open – the only naked part of him that she could see. He had a gold chain around his neck and some dark hairs on the region below the collarbone where his neck officially became his chest. She wondered if he had any scars that he would like her to see.

Joe said, 'I got to get some props ready for the girls.'

'The knife-throwing girls?'

'Uh huh.' He grinned. He gripped her bicep as if they were two men who'd just shared a pint, and he said, 'You take care of yourself, Emily.'

He walked off towards the house, leaving behind his plate and plastic cutlery. *You're not perfect, then,* thought Emily. She picked up his plate and hers, so she could tidy up, and she looked at the grease on her hands and under her fingernails. She would have been grateful for one of those individually-wrapped alcohol-soaked hand towels just then, and thinking of it made her look towards Midori, which is how she happened to be watching her friend just when it happened: There were three or four explosions from a neighbouring garden as firework rockets went off, and Emily jumped and thought about gunshots – and then Midori went down. The Japanese girl dropped, as if someone had taken hold of the edges of her and was trying to shake her down like a duvet and hadn't held on tightly enough to the corners. It didn't look as though it was something she was in control of personally. It didn't look as though she was ducking or dancing or reaching for a record from the case at her feet. It looked as though she had been shot.

Oh my God! thought Emily. *She's down!* And her next thought was that she sounded ridiculous. And then she started running towards the DJ booth, hoping that Midori was only looking for something and would pop up again in a minute and carry on. The music continued, of course, because Midori's job involved changing the records, not cranking a machine to keep them spinning round. Emily got to the booth, and Midori was on the floor, apparently unconscious. There was no blood, and she was breathing. The two Aussies, Jake and the other one, whatever his name was – the rude one – had seen what had happened and reached Midori at about the same time.

'What happened?' Jake asked Emily.

Emily said, 'I don't know. I was watching, and she just went down. She hasn't been shot?'

'What d'you reckon, Rob?' Jake said to his friend, and Rob said, 'She's fainted, mate. Maybe it was something she ate – a dodgy prawn?'

Rob took hold of Midori under the armpits and hauled her out of the DJ booth, then he shifted her up into his arms, so her chest was on his chest, and carried her with her head on his shoulder towards the house. And meanwhile Jake stepped into Midori's place, selected the next record to be played, and lined it up and mixed it in seamlessly. The music continued, and nobody who hadn't witnessed it would have known that anything had happened at all. From the nonchalant way Jake and Rob behaved, it seemed this must be a fairly regular occurrence in the outback or wherever they had grown up, something they had been drilled in, the way children on fault lines are told what to do if there is an earthquake, except that their particular fault line required that they should step in at a moment's notice to DJ at artistic parties, or carry around unconscious Japanese women in white PVC hotpants.

Emily followed Rob as he carried Midori towards a side entrance to the house, just along from the kitchen. Presumably this entrance had once been a servants' entrance. It was poorly lit and out of sight from the party, bordered by a herb garden, and what had presumably once been a vegetable patch, though it was now overgrown with weeds.

As they stepped through the mud in the dark, Emily looked over at the brightly lit front door that led directly to the grand hall. Rob must have caught her look. 'Don't want to make a fuss, eh?' he said to Emily, by way of explanation. And it was true that if he had carried Midori through the grand hall in front of all their neighbours, there would have been an awful fuss. But he tried the side door, and it wouldn't open, so then Emily tried it too. As Emily was rattling the handle, without any luck, Midori stirred a little on Rob's chest and vomited. But because Rob was pretty quick about setting her down and lying her in the recovery position and because the vomit had come out in an arc, none of it went on any of them, it just puddled into the grass.

'She's pretty crook, eh?' said Rob.

'Should I get a doctor?' said Emily.

'What about Dr. Muriel?'

Dr. Muriel was a capable woman, but she was a doctor of ethics and had no medical training, so far as Emily knew. She might have been the person to ask about whether it was any better to eat a pig than a dog or a toddler, but even if she'd been available to answer the question, this probably wasn't quite the right time to ask.

'Midori?' said Emily. And then again, 'Midori!' She said to Rob, 'I wonder if I should take her to hospital.'

Just then Midori opened her eyes and wiped her mouth with the back of her hand and said, 'Aw. Sorry about that, Rob.'

'Can you stand up?' Rob asked her.

Midori stood, a little shakily.

Rob said, 'This was gonna be your big night.'

'I know.'

'Come on, I'll get you a glass of water, and then I'll walk you home.'

'Do you want me to come?' said Emily.

'No, you're all right,' said Rob.

'It's OK, Emily,' Midori said. 'You stay at the party. I'm gonna go lie down.'

'What could have made you so ill?'

'Punch,' said Midori.

'You only had two swigs of it.'

'Well I'm glad I stayed away from it,' said Rob, 'because it must be lethal. Mate, it's really done you in.'

He took his scarf off and put it around Midori's neck. He took his jacket off and put Midori's arms into the sleeves as though she was a child who needed help getting ready for school – right arm first, that's it. Then the left. Midori was shivering. Rob put his arm around her shoulder and steered her towards home.

Emily wandered a little further up around the side of the house, away from the front door. It was quiet here – or at least, though she could hear the music, there was no one else around – and she was trying to decide whether or not she should go home or stay at the party. She felt she ought to stay and try to enjoy herself now that she didn't have to go home for Jessie. Dear old Jessie – what would she want Emily to do? Emily heard, then, the sound of a dog whimpering. Now, Emily was an imaginative person, but she wasn't suggestible, and she didn't believe in ghosts. She knew it wasn't Jessie trying to communicate with her from the afterlife. What was it, then? She decided to investigate.

She stood still and listened for a moment. The sound was coming from a cellar door a little way off to her left. She put her hand on the latch and heard it click open, and she pulled at the door. The sound of a dog in distress got louder. Emily peered in. The cellar space was vast. Clearly it was currently being used as a storage space for all the gaudy accoutrements of the performers at the house because she could see, stacked in the shadows, eight giant painted heads and other objects whose form and function was less discernible. Half a dozen fireworks exploded in the sky above her, and a little of the light reached down into the darkness and showed Emily a few bars of what seemed like a cage, and she heard the animal whimper again. What sort of brute would do something like this?

'Don't open it!' A man's voice. She turned. It was Chris.

'There's a dog down there – I can hear it whimpering.'

'So you thought you'd interfere? You didn't think it might have been put down there on purpose?'

'Yes, but seriously, why would anyone shut a dog down there in a cage in the darkness on a night like tonight?'

'You're a clever girl, Emily,' he said. 'You'll figure it out.'

He went past her – he didn't push, exactly, but he moved with intention, so that she had to step out of his way – and opened the door and went down into the cellar. Emily stood there for a moment, wondering what to do next. Then she saw Joe walking towards her out of the darkness. There seemed to be a rule tonight, that when she saw one of these two men, she'd shortly afterwards see the other – as if one always needed to be at hand to cancel the other's actions out.

'He's got a dog in there,' Emily said.

'Who? Chris?'

'You *knew* about it?'

'What can I do? He's the chief.'

'Oh my God!'

'It's one night only, Emily. It's OK.'

'It's really not.'

'Come. We can go into the house this way. Maybe you can have a drink.'

Joe walked further up the side of the house, and Emily followed him. It was very dark there. There was no path, and the only light was from the stars, the occasional firework, and whatever faint illumination reached them from the windows of the house higher up on the first and second floor. Emily stumbled and scratched her leg on some holly leaves and cursed, and Joe took her hand, matter-of-factly, so she wouldn't fall into the next bush.

She strained her eyes looking into the darkness. Was there someone else here? Up ahead of them, she heard the rustling sound of movement in the bushes. Or maybe it was the wind, or water in a stream. She thought she saw the glint of something silver – a knife? Or a bit of tinsel on a tree? She wanted to say to Joe that being in the dark was like being deep underwater, not being able to hear or turn round quickly enough to see the predator behind you. But then she scratched her leg again, and she hissed because it hurt, and then Joe stopped, so she stopped right behind him and listened to him breathing, and she didn't say anything about being underwater or what she thought she had seen.

He opened a door at the side of the house and led her into a corridor that smelled of damp stone. It was completely dark. The blackness in here trumped the blackness outside, which at least had layers and shapes in it. Joe edged forward, and Emily could tell from the way his left arm was moving that he was feeling for something in front of him – a doorway or a light. She put her hand lightly on his back and edged forward with him. 'Shh,' he said, though she hadn't said a word.

He must have reached what he'd been looking for because he stopped. A little bit of light appeared in front of them, and she could see that he had pulled at the edge of a very thick, heavy curtain until there was enough of a gap for him to peep round.

'Ach,' he said, very quietly. 'No, we're too late.'

'What is it?'

'The knife throwing.'

'We've missed it?'

'No, they're just about to start.'

'Well, can I see?'

'I suppose so. OK.'

She crouched, and he stood next to her, and they peeped through the gap in the velvet curtain like Victorian children on Christmas Eve. The sensation of standing next to him, spying on events in the grand hall, was both illicit and innocent. But just standing next to him in the darkness would have been very pleasant anyway.

The two sisters came in, to the sound of applause. 'Ah,' said Joe. And when Emily asked him, he bent down and whispered to tell her that this one was Zizi, this one was Zsa-Zsa. Apparently they were very well known; apparently they were from a famous knife-throwing family in Hungary, so Joe said, though Emily had never heard of them.

They were in their blue-grey spangly costumes, and finally Emily realised what the colour reminded her of – sharks. They were blindfolded with big, silky pale green scarves tied around their eyes. They looked vulnerable, bringing to mind the painting of *Hope* by George Frederic Watts that had hung in Emily's Nana's living room until she died, and they stood facing each other with their backs against opposite walls in a slightly recessed area of the hall that provided a natural stage. They were very close to where Emily and Joe were standing – a little too close, perhaps, if one didn't have faith in their aim – but they were a decent way away from their audience. Emily wondered if she should be worried that Joe had sounded so disappointed that he wouldn't be able to get them into the grand hall and over to the other side, and safety, before the act began.

The two sisters began to throw their ornate-handled knives simultaneously. The knives crossed mid-flight and stuck into the walls behind them, no more than two hands' width from where each sister stood. There was a pause, and then they threw again. And again, delineating an unflattering larger version of their own shapes around themselves. It was really rather exciting, and there were gasps from the audience.

The two sisters looked identical. They both had blonde hair, red lipstick, matching costumes – superficial dressing-up details that made them look the same. Emily found it harder to see the difference between them than she had when she saw them off duty upstairs in the boudoir. Perhaps it was because their features were obscured by the blindfolds. Perhaps it was the way they threw their knives with precision, at exactly the same time.

Emily was just thinking, *You know, there's got to be more than skill involved in this; there's got to be some trick; there must be some safeguard to ensure they don't hurt each other...* And then something terrible happened – one of the knives hit Zsa-Zsa in the chest. She gurgled and slumped. Her blindfold slipped. She looked towards Emily beseechingly, it seemed – although it must have been Emily's imagination because Zsa-Zsa couldn't have known Emily was there. And then she died.

Some part of Emily's brain was saying to her, *Look, don't be so unsophisticated. Just wait a few moments; this is all part of the act. This girl is going to get up and bow, and everything's going to be all right.* But people in the audience were screaming, some had started running towards the girls. The people who were furthest away, who couldn't see what had happened and who could only hear the confusion and the screaming, they reacted as though everyone in that hall must be in danger from some as yet unnamed thing – a fire, a flood, a terrorist cabal – and they started running away.

While all this was going on, the guests who were still enjoying the party in the garden outside, who either didn't want to see the knife-throwing act or who couldn't get in because it was too crowded, they were carrying on as normal; they were laughing, singing. The sound outside seemed to come in waves, as if someone was throwing it in dollops at the walls and trying to make it stick. It provided a rather sinister soundscape.

Joe had run forward towards Zsa-Zsa. Emily ran forward too, reaching for her phone. Others had got their phones out before her; others were calling the police, dialling 999. Joe was kneeling next to Zsa-Zsa, motioning at the crowd to keep back. Other performers had linked arms in front of the crowd – she saw Elise there in her belted raincoat, and the Vie en Rose people – and they were doing their best to keep order and keep everyone back, including Emily's neighbour Victoria, the mother of the skate-boarding children, who was standing there with a very non-plussed expression, arms folded, head slightly tilted to one side.

And then Emily saw something – a clue! The knife that had stuck in Zsa-Zsa's chest was not one of the ornate daggers Emily had seen upstairs in the boudoir. It was an ordinary long-handled kitchen knife. Emily looked around and above her. There were people hanging from the balconies above to look at what was going on. There were two staircases leading down into this grand hall. Anyone could have thrown that knife.

The police arrived, their radios yapping – in Brixton, you're never more than two minutes away from a squad car full of Her Majesty's finest. The place was in chaos. Behind her, Emily saw Joe dragging Zsa-Zsa away, out into the corridor where he and Emily had come in, leaving a trail of blood on the floor. Emily would have liked to intervene to tell him they didn't do it like that on TV. Shouldn't he respect the crime scene? But she felt she should get to the police and offer herself as a witness. She had been close enough to see every detail and sober enough to remember what she had seen. Even as she approached the police officers, she tried to think about what she had noticed and press it down hard into her brain, in case some little nugget of information that she laid bare turned out to be important in their enquiry. She went over it and over it like a teenager cramming for her exams: the knife was an ordinary long-handled knife, the blindfold slipped, I saw the light go out of her eyes.

'A murder has taken place!' someone announced grandly, as if they were playing the butler at a themed dinner party. At least it wouldn't be difficult to solve: there were so many, many witnesses. Though possibly none was so reliable as Emily. If she could only reach the police... She had almost got there when there was a huge burst of applause. People were grinning, looking back towards the place where Zsa-Zsa had died. Emily looked, too, and was astonished at what she saw: Zizi and Zsa-Zsa had turned up again. Zsa-Zsa had apparently died, and yet she was standing there right as rain in her bloodstained costume with the knife still sticking out of her chest. She pulled it from her costume and waved the silly stubby thing at the audience. She smiled, a strange sly smile. It was just a prop. She and her sister held hands and bowed at the audience and bowed to each other, and everyone gasped and was astonished and then clapped.

Emily looked back towards the velvet curtain, and Joe was standing there clapping vigorously, smiling away and nodding. Suddenly he didn't look so attractive, with his head wagging clownishly up and down on his neck. Emily looked towards the police officers and saw Chris talking to them. She couldn't hear what he was saying, but she could read his body language, the apology as his hands went up and he shrugged and told them the audience reaction to a performance had got out of hand.

The police officers were responding to a call on a night when every firework functions like a trick or treat for them because it sounds like a gunshot. They were busy, modern local police officers in bulletproof vests, not the tweedy Scotland Yard detectives who traditionally turn up in murder mystery stories. Nor were they career detectives in the middle of nowhere, who desperately needed this to be the murder investigation that would make their name. They were in London, soon enough there would be another stabbing. They didn't look amused, they didn't look disappointed, they didn't look as though they were going to arrest everyone for wasting police time. But elsewhere in London there were murders and knife crimes and silly children setting off fireworks – all sorts of things that had to be investigated on a very busy weekend – and they were obviously keen to leave.

So this was just another performance – a special Halloween performance for the party-goers from their new friends at the bottom of the street. It had been a fantastic theatrical trick. And yet... and yet... Emily was not so sure. She'd looked at Zsa-Zsa, and she'd watched as the light went out of her eyes. Emily had only just seen her dog die about a week before. That was the first time she'd ever seen a fellow creature die – and now it had happened again. And it was the same: Emily was sure Zsa-Zsa had died. Still, there she was, smiling and bowing.

Emily had an idea that the trick that had been performed was nastier than the one the audience thought they had seen. There were a few things that had been a little 'off' tonight. There was Zizi's rudeness in the boudoir before the performance, for example, when she had shut the door in Emily's face. But did it really amount to suspicious behaviour, or was it pre-performance nerves, a knife-thrower's right to privacy? Emily would have liked to ask Midori's opinion, but her friend was at home, sleeping off the ill effects of that glass of punch. Could Midori have been put out of the way because she had seen something in that boudoir? Had someone slipped poison into Midori's punch? If so, who? Chris had offered her a glass of punch, but so had Joe. Anyone could have put their hand over

Midori's cup while she sucked on those prawns, and dropped something nasty into it.

Emily decided to talk to Dr. Muriel and find out what Dr. Muriel made of it; she seemed like a very sensible witness-type person who could help to evaluate the facts. She wanted to talk to Joe about it. He had been standing next to her; he had dragged the 'dead' girl out of the grand hall and seen her come to life again. If it was only a trick, he'd be able to explain how it was done. Before she could talk to either of them, she had to deal with Chris. As she made her way across the grand hall, he intercepted her.

'Some trick, huh?' Chris said. 'Had me going.'

'You didn't know they were going to do it?'

'They like to keep me on my toes, those Hungarians.'

'They're Hungarian? Like Joe.'

'The name kind of gives it away: Zsa-Zsa.'

'It could be a stage name, like Midori choosing "Hana-bi".'

Chris made his funny face again. 'Midori's the name of a bright green melon liqueur. Did you know that? "DJ Melon". It's got quite a ring to it. It's half the reason I booked her for this evening, and then she told me she was going to go by "Hana-bi".'

'Chris, where's Zsa-Zsa? I need to talk to her.'

'She's around here somewhere.'

'Or Zizi – where could I find Zizi?'

'They're off duty now, Emily. I don't know. Maybe they're in one of the private rooms upstairs. Maybe they've gone to the pub.'

'Private rooms?'

'Even performers need privacy.'

Emily was going to ask him – she was going to *interrogate* him, to find out whether Midori had been poisoned for stumbling unwittingly on some secret – but Victoria came up and intervened. Victoria said, 'I heard the DJ got shot. She went down mid-set. That's what the boys said. Was she really hurt, or was it part of the act?'

Chris said, 'She got food poisoning. Apparently.'

'What we saw just now, though,' Emily said. 'The knife throwing. Was that really just an act?'

'What do you mean?' said Chris. He looked tired.

'Well, I looked at Zsa-Zsa,' said Emily, 'and her blindfold slipped after the knife went into her chest, and she looked at me, and the light went out of her eyes.'

'Really?' said Chris.

'Really!' said Victoria.

'Yes,' said Emily. 'It reminded me of when my dog died.'

Chris looked at her for a moment or two. Emily thought that perhaps he was thinking of their altercation by the cellar door and was quaking a little, taking her seriously now as a dog owner who wouldn't stand for the ill-treatment of a dog in his care. Or perhaps he was wondering if it was too late to call the police back to investigate now that Emily had come forward as a witness to tell him what she had seen. She waited to see what he would say – it would be interesting to see if he could say anything without a note of exasperation in his voice. But no... he was about to speak, and unfortunately it seemed the words were to be accompanied by a sneer.

'Does the light really go out of a creature's eyes when it dies?' Chris said. 'Really? A fish that's been out of the river for a while, yes, it gets a milky look in the eyes and a slightly fishy smell. But it's not like the soul leaving the body and curling upwards like a wisp of smoke. The light is not "in" someone's eyes in the first place. Look, I'm sorry, Emily, because you're obviously overwrought because your dog has died. But the light going out of Zsa-Zsa's eyes – it's like something in a story.'

'Where is she, then?' said Emily. 'Zsa-Zsa?'

Chris looked irritated. He said, 'She's not here.'

'She can't have just disappeared!'

'There's no mystery about it, Emily. If she wanted a break from this place, all she had to do was walk to the main road and hop on a bus.'

'All right. But I'd like to talk to Zizi.'

Chris smiled politely enough. He walked off towards the staircase without answering. Emily wondered, was he heading to the first floor boudoir to warn Zizi that Emily was on to her?

Emily stood in the middle of the grand hall and came to a decision. Yes, OK, maybe the light didn't go out of Jessie's eyes. Another way of putting it would be to say that she had ceased to be. But Zsa-Zsa had ceased to be, too – right in front of her. And dead people don't come back to life, so Emily was going to find out what was going on. Her first potential witness scurried past: Elise. She'd been standing at the front of the crowd while the knives were being thrown, and what's more, she'd be able to give Emily an insider's perspective on the relationship between Zsa-Zsa and Zizi.

'Elise!' called Emily.

Elise came over. She said, 'I need your help in a matter of the utmost importance.'

Emily said, 'I need your help, Elise. It's about the knife throwing. Can I ask you a few questions?'

Elise stood still and held up one finger. She looked at Emily. 'Could you help me get the suitcase to the gentleman?' she asked.

'Well...' said Emily.

'My name is Elise. I need to get a message to our friend, but I'm being watched. I have information that is vital, *vital*, to the success of our joint endeavour.'

'What's the message?' asked Emily.

Elise looked surprised at the question. 'Why, the message is in the suitcase.'

'OK, then. Who's it for?'

'The message is for the gentleman who is waiting for it, of course.'

'But, Elise, seriously – if that is even your real name – it's very neat that you're answering in character, but this is really real. Zsa-Zsa was your friend, wasn't she? Don't you want to help her?'

Elise said, 'Actually, no one liked her.' She said it in the same breathy voice she used for everything.

Emily looked at her for a while, and then she said, 'If I help you get the suitcase to the man, will you answer a few of my questions?'

Elise brightened. She even looked grateful. She said in a very low voice, 'I have to get the suitcase to the gentleman by the end of the evening. If there's no one to help me, I have to keep on asking.'

'So,' said Emily, 'let me get this straight. Your performance ends when you get the suitcase to the gentleman. And if I help you do that, you'll be off duty and maybe you'll answer some of my questions. OK, so where's the suitcase? Where's the gentleman?'

'The suitcase is in the nursery in the attic. The gentleman will be waiting down here, in the grand hall.'

'OK. I'll go up and get it. And what about him? Will I recognise him?'

'Yes,' said Elise. 'But be careful with the suitcase. The contents are very fragile.' Then she whirled off, very fast, running up the nearest of the two staircases in dainty dancer's shoes, presumably so she could prepare the suitcase, or at least spy on Emily to make sure she went up to the attic to keep her part of the bargain. Emily took the other staircase – why not – and headed up to the attic.

When she got to the first floor, she looked into the bedroom where she had first seen Zizi and Zsa-Zsa – how simple it would have been to have found them there and questioned them. But the place was empty. She went in and walked around; she went into the bathroom. What had Midori seen, if anything? Was it anything that someone would have poisoned her to keep her from repeating and spoiling their secret? Emily looked around the bedroom and saw only what she had seen the first time – the dressing table with the make-up and hairbrush. The bed. She looked into the cupboards and saw five identical blue-grey spangly costumes – some shabbier than others – and four pairs of matching shoes, and found that she approved that they had spares; it must make doing the laundry less stressful.

When she reached the attic, she found two doorways. One door was shut – she tried the handle, but it was locked. The other door stood open to reveal a small room in the eaves, with clean bare floorboards and an empty crib in the middle of the room. Next to it, she saw a large suitcase. It was brown leather with a metal trim. She took the handle and found that it was very heavy – she'd have been liable for an excess baggage charge if she'd tried to take it onto an aircraft, that's for sure. Before she tried to move the suitcase, she paused to take stock of her murder investigation. It was following rather a circuitous route. Still, perhaps Elise would have a useful clue. She was the only performer Emily could really talk to. Chris was sardonic and rude. Joe was... Joe was possibly implicated in covering up whatever had happened. Yes, Elise was her best chance.

Emily dragged the suitcase across the wooden floor. The sound of the metal edges of the suitcase on the wooden floor was a loud groaning protest, as if she was trying to dig a wood sprite from the knots in the floorboards. After she had managed to move the case to the doorway, she rested. After this, all she had to do was get the suitcase along the corridor and down two flights of stairs and into the grand hall in front of various assembled neighbours – and bingo, she'd be there. She put her hands on the handle and strained again to move it. She got it level with the locked door of the room next to this one. The door opened, its occupant no doubt intrigued by the dreadful noise.

'Emily?' Chris was leaning in the doorway to a sparsely furnished bedroom, legs crossed, arms folded, smiling like a model on a knitting pattern. In spite of herself, Emily peered into the room to see whether he was hiding Zsa-Zsa or Zizi in there, dead or alive. She saw a single mattress on the floor, made up comfortably with clean white sheets, a beige blanket and two fat pillows on it. She saw a straight-backed dining room chair with a pair of men's trousers and a pale blue T-shirt slung over it; a laptop computer on a very small table; and next to it, a lipstick in a gold case. The room was purely functional, a cell to sleep in – a cell for Chris to sleep in – not part of the performance space.

Chris said, 'At last! A volunteer. You're plucky, taking on the task yourself. It's heavy, isn't it? You want me to help you?'

'No, thank you,' said Emily with great dignity. When she was at school, it had always been implied that heavy lifting should be avoided because it might damage a woman's uterus. Now she hoped that if she came to grief from ignoring this advice, and the blasted thing shot out of her as she heaved at the suitcase, that at least it might land on Chris's head and choke him, mythical giant squid-like, with fallopian tentacles.

Chris smiled. He locked the bedroom door behind him and walked off down the stairs.

'Ems?' Now here was Victoria just behind Emily, doing her quizzical owl-head pose and standing in the way. 'Why don't you leave that for one of the men?'

'No, well. You see, it's a kind of performance.'

'Ooh! How clever. So it's not really heavy?'

'Well, no. It is really heavy. But I said I'd get this suitcase downstairs for Elise. The one in the raincoat?'

Fair play to Victoria, she bent down and tried to help. With both of them tugging on the handle of the suitcase, they made some progress down the corridor

till they reached the top of the staircase – but it was slow.

Why don't you get your hateful progeny to help? thought Emily.

'You know what?' said Victoria. 'Why don't we get the boys to help?' She put two fingers in her mouth and whistled. Then she shouted, 'Tommy! Jolyon! Kim!' With names like that, presumably she was hoping to get the whole bunch of them into Parliament.

'It's a question of physics,' said Emily as the boys appeared. 'Or is it geometry? Angles and levers and–'

'Why don't we just push it down the stairs?' said the middle one, Jolyon. 'Let gravity do the rest. That's physics.' He put his hands on the upturned edge of the suitcase.

'No!' said Emily. 'The contents are fragile. I have to get the suitcase to a gentleman. It's a matter of *vital importance.*'

'Yeah,' said Kim from behind his wolf mask. 'She told us that 'n' all. You know it's only a game?'

'If we put the boys in the front as buffers,' said Victoria, 'and we hold on for dear life behind...' She motioned Jolyon and Kim to take up position and

looked round for the third of her buffers, and there he was, skateboarding along the corridor in his habitual insolent pre-teen boy way.

'Well, with the skateboard,' said Emily. 'We can improvise.'

They put the skateboard, wheels up, on the banister. They laid the suitcase on the skateboard, using it like a tray. They held on and slid the thing down two flights of stairs, then they flipped the skateboard over and used it like a dolly to get the suitcase to the gentleman in the grand hall.

Emily was very grateful for the assistance of Victoria and her sons – she couldn't have done it without them – but still, it had been a tougher job than she'd bargained for when she accepted it, and she was sweating horribly by the time they arrived. She looked around for the 'gentleman', expecting to see the young man in the top hat with the rouged cheeks who had rushed past her when she first arrived at the party – or any kind of theatrical, dressed-up, amusing type. Anyone but Chris.

'Aha!' said Chris, when he saw her.

'I was looking for a gentleman,' said Emily, primly.

Chris said, 'Well, you'll have to make do with me.' He bent down and tapped at the suitcase, very gently, almost tenderly, as if its delivery really was a matter of vital importance. 'Shall I do the honours?' he said. 'Or will you?'

Emily shook her head. Really, she'd got the thing this far – why couldn't he open it? But he took a key from his pocket and handed it to her with a bow, and by then a small inquisitive crowd had gathered, so she had no choice but to smile and play her part.

She bent and put the key in the lock, Chris and Victoria and the boys arranged behind her, smiling, arms on shoulders like the Von Trapp family, and as she flipped open the lid of the suitcase, all of a sudden something lithe and large and unexpected reared up at her like a jack-in-a-box. It was Elise. She had removed her raincoat and contrived to fit her body into that suitcase – it wasn't *that* big – and had made the journey with them. She was wearing a lovely, slinky, silver 1930s dress with a tasselled fringe at the hem and at the bust. 'Thank you,' she said to Emily. She stepped over the edge of the suitcase, fitted a cigarette into a holder, lit it, and prepared to walk away.

'Wait!' said Emily. She really didn't want to go through her questions in front of Chris — but she did want an answer.

Elise knew what she wanted. She said to Emily, 'Do you know your Chekhov?'

'*The Seagull*?'

Emily had seen the same production of *The Seagull* at The Barbican in London three times in 2003. A friend of her boyfriend had had a small part in it. 'No.'

'*The Cherry Orchard*?'

Emily was not sure that she had seen *The Cherry Orchard*. She looked out in the direction of the garden and remembered the small orchard with its apple, pear and cherry trees. Perhaps it was somehow relevant? Zsa-Zsa was buried down there at the bottom of the garden under a cherry tree?

'No.'

Emily was getting uncomfortable. She saw the faces of one or two of her neighbours in the crowd — the young black man who was always repairing his car. The Indian woman with the disabled parking space and the herb garden at the front of her house. Emily hoped they would think it was part of the show. She said to Elise, 'You'll have to give me a clue.'

'You really don't know?' Elise gave Emily a look of such contempt. Then she walked away.

'Do you need me to help you?' asked Chris.

'I really don't,' said Emily. Then she walked away too.

'Don't miss the parade,' called Chris. 'We're burning a witch.'

Somebody laughed. Then behind her, she heard the small crowd break into polite applause. Someone whistled – the chap who was always repairing his car, perhaps. Emily didn't look back.

Emily wanted to find Joe. She went out into the garden and saw him standing there, tall and handsome, easy to spot in the crowd. She went towards him as quickly as she could. Joe and Emily. With their very English names they could have been toddlers playing up while their mothers had a natter in Starbucks, except that Joe was so tall and so handsome and so Hungarian, and Emily was... Emily was sweating like an adult woman who has just lugged a suitcase containing a contortionist down two flights of stairs.

'That was mad,' she said. She meant the knife throwing, but she could have been talking about any of it.

Joe smiled, as though it was a compliment. 'They've lit the bonfire,' he said. 'Come and sit over here, or you'll smell as though you're forged in a volcano.' He took her hand and led her over to one of the wooden benches. They sat there for a moment. Joe seemed as exhausted as if he had personally raised Zsa-Zsa from the dead. If only that was a legitimate possible explanation. Emily looked around at the other guests in the garden, trying to decide what she wanted to ask him. Was she really going to ask him if he had just covered up a death? Perhaps the knife had slipped, and out of loyalty...

'Wait here,' Joe said. She must have looked as though she hadn't said what she'd come out here to say because he put his hand on her shoulder and said, 'I won't be long. I'll come back.'

'Do you know your Chekhov?' said Emily.

'What can you mean?'

'It's something Elise said. It's about Zsa-Zsa. I need to know the names of the plays.'

Maybe he looked at her strangely, and maybe he didn't. It was hard to see in the darkness with the smoke from the bonfire blowing in their eyes.

'No,' he said. 'I don't know anything.' He walked away.

Emily sat and waited. Not far from where she was sitting, the little stall was still going, serving roast pig straight from the spit. Emily spotted a very elderly lady she knew heading for the front of the long queue of people waiting to be served with a slice of pork. Emily only knew this lady as 'Auntie'. It was a term of respect rather than an acknowledgement of familial ties because Auntie was originally from Jamaica and Emily had never even been there on holiday. Auntie was small, but she was mighty. She was fierce. She stood in her slippers at the gate post in front of her house most days and greeted the world as it passed by. The gate post was only a few feet from her front window, so there was no doubt that she stood there not because she'd get a better view but because she wanted to hail the passersby and get a greeting in return.

Seeing the long queue for the roast pork, rather than wasting time trying to evaluate how long it would take her to wait and whether or not she should stand in line or come back, Auntie had taken the sensible decision to press her suit as one of the oldest people there and had walked to the front and held out her plate.

'Hello, Auntie,' Emily called.

Auntie gave a queenly wave, but she didn't look back. She was concentrating on her plate as the meat piled up on it. 'A liccle more,' she said to the man in the chef's hat each time he paused. 'A liccle more.'

Now Dr. Muriel was heading in Emily's direction, her cane in one hand, a cup of punch in the other. 'I wonder if it's true,' Emily said to her, 'that roast pork smells like roasting human flesh.'

She'd thought Dr. Muriel would say something obvious like, 'Let's hope we never find out!' Instead she said, 'When is something "true", Emily? Is it when you read about it or hear about it, when you see it with your own eyes – or is there some other term of reference for you?'

'In this case,' said Emily. 'I'd have to smell it with my own nose, wouldn't I?'

Dr. Muriel sat down next to Emily, as though Emily had been waiting for her. So Emily took advantage of the situation to expound her theories about the knife throwing.

'No one has seen Zsa-Zsa since the knife throwing. Did she die right in front of me? Was she stabbed afterwards? Or is she alive?'

'It might have been an accident,' said Dr. Muriel. 'Seems like a night for mishaps. A girl just set herself on fire over there by the house. One of the performers. A silly girl with a cigarette holder and a silver flapper dress. The fringe of her dress went up, whoosh! Luckily for her your friend whatshisname, Sonny Jim, he was there to smother the flames.'

Was he? Emily thought of Joe, heroic and strong, wrestling Elise to the ground to save her from burning– and hopefully bruising her a bit in the process.

She said, 'It could have been anyone at the party who threw that knife.'

'But if Zsa-Zsa died, then who was it who came back again to show us that it was a prop? To show us that she *hadn't* been killed with a knife? You're not saying they did something with mirrors? Or videotape? I was watching, and I saw that girl come back, large as life.'

'So we have suspects,' Dr. Muriel said. 'But no murder. That's interesting. That's a conundrum. "Remember, remember, the 5th of November. Gunpowder, treason and plot." How very apt that you should be investigating a murder that may not have happened, on Bonfire Night, a night which celebrates a regicide that never happened. You need a motive, don't you? Though before you start with that, I'd say you need to have a murder.'

'I've got a murder – I've just got to convince everyone else.'

'All right then, m'dear. You need a body. If there's been a murder, there will be a body.'

'You're right. I need to find one. And if I can't find one, I can at least look.'

'Flower beds? Anything recently dug up.'

'It's just a tangle of weeds everywhere. Nothing has been touched for twenty years.'

'The bonfire? You couldn't really tuck a body in there without the whole lot falling down like a pile of fiddlesticks.'

'Let me think.' Emily closed her eyes to concentrate, and instead of seeing where they might have hidden the body, she thought of Jessie. Even at the end, when everything else had gone – sight, hearing, back legs and sphincter – Jessie could smell a gravy bone across the kitchen. She'd have enjoyed the game of hunting for Zsa-Zsa, even if it was rather a ghoulish game. And as Emily thought of Jessie, it was almost as though the dog was helping her with her enquiries (only almost because, of course, she didn't believe in ghosts), and she thought about that cellar with the poor dog in a cage down there. A dark cellar would be a very good place to hide a body.

She opened her eyes and looked towards the side of the house where the cellar was situated. She could see Joe arguing with Chris and Zizi up by the locked side door to the house where Midori had vomited.

'I feel that I'm going about this the wrong way,' Emily said to Dr. Muriel. 'I should just ask Joe. Or Zizi. Or any of them. I should ask them straight out.'

'Indeed,' said Dr. Muriel. 'But you won't know what to ask them unless you find a body. If it was just a jolly good trick, they won't tell you their professional secrets, will they?'

'If there's been a murder, I don't suppose they'll confess. Who'd want to admit to killing someone?'

'You'd be surprised,' said Dr. Muriel. 'There are boastful people, frightened people, and those who just want to unburden themselves. You know, in my line of work, I enquire into all sorts of tricky situations, and after a while, one starts to see that there is no absolute right and wrong. There is only what might be and what must be. One quickly adjusts to the idea that in certain situations, for certain people, it would be no trouble at all to kill someone.'

Emily stood and looked down for a moment on Dr. Muriel's meaty-looking shoulders and that cane with the silver head on it. 'Assuming that's not a confession,' she said, 'I'll go and look in the cellar. Unless you want to save me the trouble and tell me where you hid the body?'

Dr. Muriel laughed and waved her cane. Emily set off towards the cellar – and Joe.

'Was that Zizi you were talking to?' she asked Joe. There was no sign of Chris or Zizi. Or Zsa-Zsa.

'She's not very happy with me,' he said. He looked embarrassed.

'I'm going to the cellar, Joe. I think Zsa-Zsa may be in there.'

'Really? You think Chris locked her in there with that dog? He's not such a bad man as you make out.'

'I saw the three of you arguing. I wish I could talk to Zizi.'

'She's leaving,' said Joe. 'Maybe she already left.'

'Just Zizi?'

'They're leaving. Isn't that what I said? Their mother is sick in Hungary. She has Alzheimer's. They have to go back.'

'The thing is, Joe...' How to put this? 'I really want to know what happened tonight. You dragged a dead body out of there after the knife throwing. And then, miraculously, she seemed to come to life.'

'What you talking about, Emily?'

'I told you about my dog?'

'Emily, tonight you told everybody.'

'She was old, and I knew she was going to die. I was really worried about it. I hoped that she would die in her sleep. But she got more and more frail, and more and more old, and in the end I had to get the vet to come round. And it was actually a peaceful death – so much so that, in my emotional state, I felt that I could almost enjoy going round with the vet, from house to house, watching as animals are killed peacefully.' Emily was getting a bit off-track here. 'But of course, that sounds a bit weird. What I mean, Joe, is that I watched as she died. And she just ceased to be.'

Not surprisingly, Joe looked bemused. 'I'm sorry about your dog, Emily.'

'I watched and saw exactly the same thing with Zsa-Zsa. I know she died. So what happened? Was it an accident? Did Zizi throw inaccurately? Did someone throw a kitchen knife from the balcony?'

'It was a stunt, Emily. But Zizi threw a bit hard. Her sister fainted. I pinched her ears in the corridor, and she stood up and took her bow.'

'You pinched her ears?'

Joe smiled. He leaned forward and took hold of the outer edge of her left ear with his right hand. He didn't pinch it. He touched her, and then he let go. 'Try it,' he said. 'It really works. You know?'

'Zsa-Zsa fainted?'

'It was a bit emotional. They had a row today.'

'Ah. I thought so.'

'They look identical. When a man's tired... When a man's tired and a girl gets into bed with him...

Maybe the sister plays a trick, and it gets out of hand.'

'Chris! The weasel! I saw that lipstick in his bedroom. I can't believe I missed such an obvious clue. He slept with both of them? No wonder they were angry.'

'Emily, maybe it's not the man's fault.'

'It's always the man's fault, Joe. So Zizi killed her? She stabbed her sister out of jealousy? I'd been trying to find a motive – people smuggling, drugs, diamonds...'

Joe had been looking worried but he laughed at Emily's list. 'Emily, nothing happened. There wasn't a murder.'

'I saw it happen.'

'I know you feel sad about your dog. Everything doesn't relate back to that. You know?'

'And Chris is implicated. I know you're covering up for them, but you'll get in trouble if you don't go to the police, Joe.'

'But somebody already called the police – they came here and saw for themselves there wasn't a murder.'

'Yes. That's the clever bit. Now if we call again and tell them what happened, they'll never believe us. We need evidence. All I have is theories, but I *know* Chris put something in Midori's drink and poisoned her. He set fire to Elise because she tried to give me a clue.'

'Chris set fire to Elise?'

'Dr. Muriel told me. Her dress caught fire, and Chris was there. I thought she was talking about you, but she meant Chris. Setting fire to someone or smothering the flames – to an onlooker, there's very little difference. He was giving Elise a warning, telling her to keep silent. He's dangerous, Joe. You be careful.'

'Emily, I tell you what. I think you're crazy, but I'll talk to Chris. I'll talk to Zizi. I'll see if I can find Zsa-Zsa. Will that do?'

But Emily was distracted. Up ahead in the darkness, near the house, she could just about make out Dr. Muriel skirting past the bushes. She was heading for the cellar. 'You see what you can find out,' Emily said to Joe. 'I'm sorry. I've got to go.'

Before Emily could reach her, Dr. Muriel had opened the cellar door and gone inside. Emily followed, hating the darkness. This was the king of darkness compared to the ill-lit passageway that led here and the corridor that looked on to the grand hall. This was a spidery darkness, full of stacked things and shadows – and, presumably, Dr. Muriel.

'Emily?' Dr. Muriel's voice was behind her. A light flared in the cellar, showing the row of giant faces painted on fibreglass heads as big as a person, each one with different features, but similar in construction to the glowing heads Emily had seen in the garden when she first arrived. She looked for the cage with the dog in it, but it had gone.

'Dr. Muriel?' Emily called. 'Is it just you in here?'

'Come and look at this, m'dear.'

Emily went back towards the cellar door. She saw a thin beam of light from a pen torch on a key ring as Dr. Muriel shone it on a painted sarcophagus, depicting a larger than life-size pink naked woman with long black hair and big blue eyes, her nudity innocent as a mermaid's, though from what Emily could see of it, she had legs. Dr. Muriel tapped, like an electrician tapping at panelling to check whether the space behind it is hollow and might contain wires that could kill if someone drills into them. She pulled at a catch on the side of the lady, just about where her ribs would be, and lifted the lid upwards to reveal another painted lady inside. It was Zsa-Zsa, the kitchen knife still in her chest, her pretty face tinged with a blue that matched her costume.

'I know what you said about right and wrong,' Emily said. 'But until you see something like this, you can't really believe it.'

Dr. Muriel said, 'Sometimes people are driven to do terrible things.'

And then, as if proof were needed – which it was not – Emily felt the business end of Dr. Muriel's cane on the back of her head, and she went down in a lump.

A short while later, Emily regained consciousness. She was standing upright, and her legs were untethered, but her arms were pinioned. She was in darkness, her upper body enclosed in a roughly spherical space. The air that she breathed had the smell of an art room about it. From outside, roast pork and bonfire smokiness drifted into the cellar – she couldn't have been unconscious for too long. It was still the night of the party.

'Emily,' called Dr. Muriel, fairly robustly, considering the circumstances, 'what is this? A pantomime horse.'

'I think you might be inside a giant head. You didn't whack me, did you, with your cane?'

'No, of course not! You really are a most suspicious girl.'

'Dr. M., what do you know about Chekov?'

'Ah, well.' Dr. M cleared her throat as if to start on a very long lecture. Her voice echoed slightly in her improvised prison. 'The Russians, of course–'

'I mean, tell me the name of some Chekov plays.'

'*The Seagull*. I think that might be my favourite because–'

'Dr. Muriel, can you just give me a list?'

'*The Seagull, The Cherry Orchard, Uncle Vanya*... I could tell you a rather amusing story about the time I saw *Uncle Vanya* in–'

'Please don't.'

'*Three Sisters*.'

So that was it. '*Three sisters*!' Emily said. 'It seems obvious now, doesn't it? It's simple arithmetic. If two are alive and one is dead...'

An arc of light swung through the darkness in the cellar – Emily could see it through the peepholes in the head, which were located in the nostrils that had been painted on the face. She looked for the painted sarcophagus, but she couldn't see it. She couldn't see who was in the cellar with them – whether rescuer or assailant. 'Shh,' she whispered to Dr. Muriel. 'I think we're not alone.'

'What's that, m'dear? SPEAK UP!' said Dr. Muriel.

The light swung again. This time Emily had a chance to see who was there – it was Chris. He held a powerful torch, which he put on the ground in front of him. Now he was standing just in front of her with an axe in his hand. Emily tried to determine whether she should run for her life (and look ridiculous) or stay still or aim a good kick at him and hope he didn't chop her legs off.

'Emily!' said Chris. 'Nice head. Is this going to be another performance?'

She said, 'Don't do anything stupid, Chris. The police know I'm here.'

'Of course they do.' He came up very close, his eye to her peephole.

'Chris!' shouted Dr. Muriel from inside her giant head. 'Is that you?'

Chris turned at the sound of Dr. Muriel's voice and swung his axe violently.

'No!' screamed Emily. She shut her eyes in spite of herself. She opened them again to see through the nostril peepholes that he was coming for her now. He swung his axe. The fibreglass prison split open. She stepped free; she was unharmed. She looked to her left, and Dr. Muriel was there, also unharmed. Their well-being seemed to provide yet another clue to the case, which Emily tried to process.

Chris took Emily's hand and pulled her towards him. He looked as if he was going to hug her.

'Where's the dog that was down here?' asked Emily.

'My dog? Sam. He was frightened of the fireworks, so I put him down here out of the way. Honestly, Emily, he lives like a prince the rest of the time. It was for one night, and it was for his own good. But OK, you made me feel guilty, so I put him up in my room.'

'Where's that sarcophagus?' said Dr. Muriel. 'The painted lady? Zsa-Zsa's in it.'

'If you mean the witch that was in here, she's part of the parade. They're going to put her on the bonfire and burn her. Seriously, you think Zsa-Zsa's in it? It's supposed to be empty.'

Dr. Muriel said, 'Chris, we know she's in it. We've seen her.'

They scrambled out of the cellar. Out in the garden, the parade had already started. It was an ethereally beautiful sight: A procession of six giant heads lit from inside seemed to float towards the bonfire, flanked by eight Polish stilt-walkers in top hats and coattails, juggling flaming torches. It all looked desperately dangerous – but these people were about to burn (albeit unwittingly) the body of a young woman who had been murdered a few hours before, so it seemed ridiculous to cavil about Health and Safety.

At the front of the procession, Emily saw the sarcophagus being carried on the shoulders of a couple of men. The distance between the house and the bonfire wasn't that great, but the performers were making the most of it by covering the width as well as the length of the garden, winding from one side of it to the other very slowly, weaving around the fruit trees in the orchard. Now they were heading back. The garden was packed with spectators. Some stood on the wooden benches and applauded; others surrounded the performers, pressing in to get a good look. A few – the kids, mostly –joined the back of the parade.

'Stop!' yelled Chris. But the music was too loud. Nobody heard him

'But who knocked us out in the cellar?' Dr. Muriel asked Chris as they pressed through the crowd towards the bonfire. 'And why didn't the performers notice us as they brought the heads out, or at least notice they were only bringing out six giant heads instead of eight of them for the parade?'

'The props guy was supervising.'

'Joe?' asked Emily.

'Yes, Joe.'

'Joe set this up?'

Chris said, 'I don't know if he set it up or he was covering up. He's pretty resourceful. I guess if he knew Zsa-Zsa was dead, he presumed the person who killed her was Zizi. He's in love with Zizi.'

Emily was slightly out of breath from the running and jostling. By now she and Chris were about halfway between the front and the back of the parade. They had left Dr. Muriel behind. Emily was panting as she said, 'Joe was involved with Zizi? But I saw her lipstick in your bedroom.'

'Did you? Boy, you're nosey. It must have been Zsa-Zsa's. The sisters weren't speaking to each other before the performance. I had to let Zsa-Zsa get ready upstairs in my room. For a while there we thought she wasn't even going to go on.'

'So the sister I saw in the boudoir was the third sister? No wonder they didn't look identical – just similar.'

Chris said, 'I don't know, Emily. You're the detective.'

The parade had reached the bonfire. People had begun chanting. 'Burn the witch! Burn the witch!' Chris and Emily had pushed their way to the front – Auntie would have been proud.

'Stop!' yelled Chris again. He and Emily leapt on the two men who were carrying Zsa-Zsa in her colourful coffin. As she wrapped her arms and legs around him to tackle him, Emily was sorry – but not surprised – to discover that one of the men was Joe.

As it was knocked to the ground, the lid of the sarcophagus sprang open, and there was Zsa-Zsa: bluish, beautiful, dead, with the knife in her chest.

'Call the police,' someone said. It might have been Emily.

Emily disengaged herself from Joe. After she and Chris had toppled him, she had lain, briefly, on top of Joe, her knees tucked up (but clasped demurely together) at about the level of his waist, her head tucked under his chin, her ear on his throat – like a very tired or frightened young monkey clinging for comfort to its mother.

'I'm sorry, Emily,' said Joe, as he stood up. A Polish stilt-walker grabbed his shoulders, and Ravi from Emily's local shop held on to his elbows. But Joe offered no resistance.

Dr. Muriel caught up with them, ploughing through the crowd with elbows and cane before her, giving a knock to anyone who didn't get out of the way. Emily turned her friend right round again and walked with her back to the house.

'So the third sister turned up in London last night and asked one of them or both of them to go back to Hungary with her to help with the sick mother?' said

Dr. Muriel as they made their way through the scandalised crowd, which by now was buzzing with news of the discovery of Zsa-Zsa's body.

'It seems so. But there was an argument, and Zizi refused to leave Joe, so Zsa-Zsa set him up and got into bed with him so her sister would think they'd been sleeping together and get angry.'

'Well, certainly she got angry. That was quite a betrayal.'

'Yes. But the plan backfired, and Zizi refused even to let Zsa-Zsa get ready in the same bedroom, and Zsa-Zsa threatened that she wasn't going to perform. So Zizi put the third sister in one of the shabby spare costumes in case she had to go on.'

'A bit of a risk – if she was out of practice, we might have ended up with a different dead body.'

'They're from a famous knife-throwing family, apparently. Very well known in Hungary. Besides, I expect they could see through the blindfolds. Anyway, then... I don't know. Zsa-Zsa insisted on doing the performance, I suppose. And instead of using the sawn-off prop, Zizi threw a real kitchen knife and killed her.'

Dr. Muriel stopped and rested on her cane and looked up at the dark passageway that led past Midori's long-since-absorbed vomit puddle towards the side doors and the cellar. 'And the third sister was waiting outside in the bushes?'

'She must have been. You know, I thought I saw someone – or heard them. It was just a glinting and a bit of rustling. You know something else? When Zsa-Zsa died and she looked towards the curtain, she must have seen Joe. I thought she was looking beseechingly at me, but it must have been him. Maybe the light didn't go out of her eyes. But I know a beseeching look when I see one.'

'So Joe dragged Zsa-Zsa's body away from the grand hall, and the third sister stepped in to take the bow.'

'Yes. But whether she was in on it or she was just protecting Zizi, I have no way of knowing.'

'I suppose it will all come out in court,' said Dr. Muriel, sagely.

'One good thing about this evening,' said Emily. 'I didn't learn personally whether roast pig smells like a roast person.'

'And you let go of Jessie.'

'Hmm,' said Emily. 'Not quite.'

Chris caught up with them just before they reached the front door of the house. He must have been running because he looked flushed. He took Emily's hand, and he got a look on his face that made his nose seem longer and straighter than usual. Emily recognised it finally for what it was: shyness. It twisted his mouth so it looked kind of sexy.

He said, 'Would you consider joining us, Emily? You've got a lovely loud shrieking voice; you were very game with that suitcase. You're tenacious; you're good at remembering things. You'd be, you know, an asset.'

Emily looked at him and thought that this might be the offer that would help her, finally, to forget Jessie, to let go and move on from her old life. 'Thank you,' said Emily. 'But no.'

The flashing blue lights and the protesting 'not ME, not ME, not ME' sound of the sirens announced that the police had arrived and were parking up on the road outside. Chris left Emily, with a somewhat reluctant final squeeze of her hand, and went off to deal with them.

'I'll walk you back to your flat, dear,' said Dr. Muriel to Emily. 'If you don't mind stopping by the kitchen first so I can pick up my trolley.'

As they walked together back to the house, Dr. Muriel said, 'I don't suppose we shall ever discover whether Midori was poisoned – but for what it's worth, I very much doubt it. That girl was overexcited and wearing very constricting clothing, and she bolted her food from what you told me, and she drank that punch down straight. It sounds like what my mother would have called a giddy spell – she was a classic candidate. Other than that, Emily, is there any aspect of this case left unresolved?'

'Well, I did wonder,' said Emily, 'whether Joe *really* liked my cheesy potato bake that I brought.'

'I don't know about that, m'dear,' said Dr. Muriel. 'But if it's pertinent to the case, I'm sure it will come out in court.'

By the same author:

ALISON WONDERLAND
Only occasionally does a piece of fiction leap out and
demand immediate cult status. Alison Wonderland
is one.
The Times

Smith is gin-and-tonic funny.
Booklist

BEING LIGHT
Smith has a keen eye for material details, but her
prose is lucid and uncluttered by heavy description.
Imagine a satire on Cool Britannia made by the Coen
Brothers.
Times Literary Supplement

This is a novel in which the ordinary and the unusual
are constantly juxtaposed in various idiosyncratic
characters... Its airy quirkiness is a delight.
The Times

A screwball comedy that really works.
The Independent

By the same author:

THE MIRACLE INSPECTOR
The Miracle Inspector is one of the few novels that everyone should read, it's a powerful novel that's masterfully written and subtly complex.
SciFi and Fantasy Books

Helen Smith crafts a story like she's the British lovechild of Kurt Vonnegut and Philip K. Dick.
Journal of Always Reviews

About the author:

 Helen Smith is a novelist and
playwright who lives in London.
She is the author of Alison
Wonderland, Being Light and
The Miracle Inspector as well as
the Emily Castles mysteries.